STORIES
THAT MAKE
A DIFFERENCE

Inspirational Anecdotes Worth Sharing Again

Collected By

Wayne Soares

ISBN: 978-0-9963736-6-1

Copyright 2017 by Wayne Soares

For more information, visit www.SummerlandPublishing.com.

Printed in the U. S. A.

Library of Congress   2016963060

DEDICATION

To my beautiful daughter, Jessie.
You are the rose that continuously blossoms in my life.

ACKNOWLEDGMENT

Many thanks to Jolinda Pizzirani for her layout and cover design efforts, and to Anya Petersen-Frey for her publishing guidance and assistance.

FORWARD

Stories That Make a Difference will change your perspective on life. Wayne Soares has a gift that very few writers have. His writing matches his uplifting personality. He can make you laugh and cry and look at yourself in the mirror even when there's no mirror around.

This book makes you a better person. Not only is the reading fun, you can't wait to learn from the next story. It's a "must read" for adults and children and anyone in between. *Stories That Make a Difference* is a perfect read for today's world.

Steve Burton
Sports Broadcaster
WBZ TV, CBS Boston

OPENING

Give me such courage and I can scale the hardest and highest peaks alone, and transform every stumbling block into a stepping stone.

> *-Gale Brook Burket*

INTRODUCTION

Several years ago, my 6-year old daughter wanted to come with me to a golf tournament I was scheduled to play in. She said, "Daddy, I can be your caddy."

To which I replied, "I don't know honey, it's a long day, plus you'll have to count my swings at the ball."

"I can do that!" she confidently exclaimed.

I said, "OK, how much is 6+6+9?"

"FIVE" she yelled.

"Okay, let's go!!!!!!" I said.

It is my hope that the following stories will inspire you, motivate you and bring laughter into your life.

A short, simple story about Teamwork

A man falls into a hole. Three hours go by until he sees a doctor. The man asks the doctor for help and the doctor writes a prescription and throws it down in the hole.

Two more hours go by when a priest looks down the hole and sees the man. "Can you help me father?" the man says.

The priest says a prayer and leaves. One hour goes by and the man's best friend looks down the hole. Seeing his buddy in the hole, his pal jumps in.

The man says, "Are you crazy? Now we're both stuck in this hole!"

His best friend looks at him and says, "Don't worry, I've been in here before. And I know the way out.

EMPATHY

There is a classroom of 4th grade students, all doing their work. A nine-year old boy is sitting at his desk when all of a sudden there is a puddle between his feet and the front of his pants are all wet. He has no idea how this has happened and he is horribly afraid of being laughed at by the girls and boys in his class.

The boy puts his head down and is filled with embarrassment and soon-to-be humiliation. He can just hear his classmates laughing and teasing him and his heart is aching. He raises his head and sees his teacher coming towards him – HE HAS BEEN DISCOVERED!!

As the teacher is approaching him, his classmate Susie is carrying a goldfish bowl filled with water. She trips in front of the teacher and accidentally dumps the bowl of water in the boy's lap.

The boy pretends to be angry but is totally relieved to have the attention away from him. Now, instead of being the object of ridicule, the boy is the object of immediate sympathy. The teacher takes the boy to the gym to change into shorts while his pants dry.

All the other children are cleaning up around the desk. But as luck would have it, the boy escapes the verbal abuse and it is transferred in a flash to someone else – Susie. She tries to help but the children tell her to go away and that she is too clumsy. She puts her head down and slowly returns to her desk.

At the end of the day as everyone is waiting for their bus, the boy sees Susie and walks over to her and whispers, "Why did you spill water on me?"

To which Susie whispers back, "I wet my pants once too."

LOVE

It was a busy morning, about 8 am, when an elderly gentleman in his early 80's arrived at the hospital to have stitches removed from his thumb. He said he was in a hurry as he had an appointment at 9 am.

The nurse took his vital signs and told him to take a seat, knowing it would be over an hour before the doctor was able to see him. The man kept looking at his watch and the nurse, since she was not busy, decided to evaluate the old man's wound. After examining it, she saw it was so well healed she spoke to one of the doctors and got the needed supplies to remove his stitches and clean the wound.

While taking care of his thumb, the nurse asked the man if he had another doctor's appointment this morning because he kept checking his watch. The old gentleman said no but that he needed to go to the nursing home to eat breakfast with his wife.

The nurse asked him what kind of health she was in. The man said that she had been there for a while and that she was the victim of Alzheimer's disease. The nurse inquired if his wife would be upset if he were late today.

The man replied that she no longer knew who he was and that she had not recognized him in over 5 years now.

The nurse was quite surprised and asked the gentleman, "Even though she doesn't know who you are, you still go every morning?"

The old man smiled and patted the nurse's hand and said, "She doesn't know me, but I still know who she is."

The happiest of people don't necessarily have the best of everything; they make the best of everything they have.

KINDNESS

The cabdriver arrived at the address and honked the horn. After waiting a few minutes, he walked to the door....

"Just a minute please," answered the frail, elderly voice.

After a long pause, the door opened. A small woman in her 90's stood before the cabdriver. She was wearing a print dress and a pillbox hat with a veil pinned on it. She looked like she came right out of a 1940's movie.

By the woman's side was a small, nylon suitcase. The apartment looked as if nobody had lived in it for years. All the furniture was covered with sheets. There were no clocks on the walls, no knickknacks or utensils on the counter. In the corner was a cardboard box filled with photos and glassware.

The woman asked the cabbie if he could take her bag out of the car, and he was happy to assist her. She took his arm and they walked slowly to the cab. She kept thanking the man for his kindness and he told her that he treated all his passengers this was.

She said, "Oh, you're such a good boy." She got in the cab and gave the man an address and then asked if she could drive through town.

The cabbie told her it wasn't the shortest way and she replied, "Oh, I don't mind. I'm in no hurry, I'm on my way to hospice.

As she began to speak, the man looked in the rear-view mirror and saw that the woman's eyes were glistening. "I don't have any family left," she said in a soft voice. "The doctors say I don't have very long left."

The cabbie reached up and shut off the meter. "What route would you like me to take?" he asked.

For the next two hours, they drove through the city. The woman showed the cabbie where she had once worked as an elevator operator. They drove through the neighborhood where she and her husband had lived when they were newlyweds. She had the cabbie pull up in front of the old furniture warehouse that had once been a ballroom where she had gone dancing as a girl.

Sometimes, she'd ask the man to slow down in front of a particular building or corner and would sit, staring into the darkness, saying nothing.

As the first hint of sun was creasing the horizon, she suddenly said, "I'm tired. Let's go now. They drove in silence to the address she had given him. It was a low building that looked like a convalescent home.

Two orderlies came out to the cab as the cab pulled up. They were kind and pleasant and watched her every move. They were expecting her. When the cabbie opened the trunk to get her things, the women was already seated in the wheelchair. When asked what she owed for the fare, the man replied, "Nothing."

The woman answered, "Oh, but you have to make a living." The cabbie said that he had other passengers and bent down, without thinking, gave the woman a hug. She held on tightly and whispered, "You gave an old woman a little moment of joy today. "Thank you so much."

The cabbie squeezed her hand and then walked back to his car, hearing the door shut behind him. He didn't pick up any more passengers on his shift and drove around lost in thought. For the rest of the day, he could hardly talk. After thinking to himself, he realized that he had never done anything more important in life.

Great moments in life, sometimes catch us unaware.

People may not remember exactly what you did or what you said, but they will always remember how you made them feel.

THE IMPORTANCE OF LIFE

The policeman waited in his car for about 30 seconds after he had just pulled over a speeding vehicle. The man nonchalantly got out of the car and approached the police cruiser.

"Hey Bob, fancy meeting you like this" he said with a nervous laugh. "First time I've ever been caught in the last five years" (he was lying through his teeth).

The officer recognized his next-door neighbor and said, "Sam, you have a reputation in our precinct of having a very heavy foot." Sam's smile disappeared. "Please wait in the car, Sam."

As Sam went back to his car he slammed the door. He couldn't believe that his next-door neighbor, the same guy that went to his church, was going to give him a ticket. "I'm NEVER talking to that bum again" Sam fumed.

Ten, fifteen, twenty minutes went by. What could Bob be doing Sam thought? Finally, after twenty-five minutes Bob emerged from his cruiser and knocked on Sam's car window. He opened it just enough so Bob could slide the piece of paper in through the window. "THANKS!" Sam snapped.

Bob said nothing and returned to his cruiser and drove off. Sam was surprised to find, not a ticket, but a note. It read:

Dear Sam:

Several years ago, my little six-year-old daughter was killed by a speeding driver as she rode her bike down this road. The man received ten years and was out after three for good behavior. He got to go home to his three daughters. I have to wait til I get to heaven before I see my little girl again. PLEASE slow down Sam. I have an 11-year old boy and he's all that I've got left.

Thanks,

Bob

Life is so precious. It's what we make of it. We can go through it being miserable, judgmental and angry or we can appreciate what we have every single day. No matter how big or how small.

FRIENDSHIP

Jimmy Porter was a very popular kid. As an 8th grader, he had very unique qualities that come along once in a great while; a wonderful personality, leadership skills and the ability to make others feel comfortable.

His peers looked up to him and his teachers marveled at what a special, young boy he was. He also possessed the combination of being a fine student-athlete. Bigger than his peers, Jimmy commanded instant respect from everyone at the junior high school, and, he had a tremendously, caring heart.

Quite uncommon for a person his age.

During recesses, it was Jimmy who picked the teams and divided the up equally. It was Jimmy who would always take the less-talented kid on his team. Alex was not a very good kickball player but he knew that Jimmy would certainly pick him on his team and encourage him when he needed it. It was Jimmy that would invite the less popular kids to sit at his table during lunch and it was Jimmy who would immediately stick up for someone if they were being bullied. Rather than ignore it, Jimmy was willing to take a stand against anyone.

He received his first encounter with bullies in the 4th grade on the playground. Jimmy was playing basketball when he stopped and saw three boys teasing a girl to the point of tears. Her name was Amanda and she came from a very poor family. She was constantly verbally abused because of her clothes and appearance.

The boys were calling her a "dirt bag" and spitting at her. Jimmy dropped the basketball and raced towards them. His pals followed in close pursuit. He got in one of their faces, causing the other two to freeze in their tracks. "You sicken me, you punk" said Jimmy through clenched teeth. "Go ahead, spit at me.... spit at me."

He moved closer to the other two boys. "DO NOT ever come near this girl again. Do you hear me?" They nodded. Then took off to the other side of the playground.

Jimmy truly felt sorry for the girl. She seemed helpless. How could anybody be that mean he thought. From that day forward, he and Amanda became good pals. They sat together at lunch and on the bus and helped each other with their homework.

Now in 8th grade, Amanda had turned into a beautiful girl and was one of the best runners and field hockey players in the entire school. Without question, Jimmy Porter was a special young man.

It was Friday, September 20th. School had been in session for almost three weeks and Jimmy was on his way to the bus stop. It would be a day that he would remember for the rest of his life.

As he got on the bus, he walked to the back and sat in his seat. Jimmy's mind was on baseball practice after school. Next week was their first game and he was quite happy about how good his team was going to be this season. When the bus arrived at school, Jimmy got off and went to stand with a few of his teammates, Bobby, TJ and Sam. There was the usual kidding and banter back in forth. The kind you would expect from close knit friends.

"Got a big math test today" said Jimmy.

"Mrs. Kelly gives the hardest tests" TJ chipped in.

"Yeah, she's brutal. I barely got 70% on my last test" offered Bobby.

"It couldn't be that Karen Jenkins sits right next to you and you couldn't concentrate, now couldn't THAT be the case?" asked TJ mischievously.

"I'm NOT interested in Karen Jenkins!" said Bobby embarrassingly.

"Yeah, yeah. OK L-O-V-E-R-B-O-Y!" said Jimmy.

"Look out for those arrows pal" said Sam.

"What arrows?" inquired Bobby.

"Cupid's!" yelled Jimmy. Bobby made a face and they all laughed as the bell rang for the start of the school day.

Around mid-morning, Jimmy's teacher asked him if he would deliver something to the main office for her. Since his class was on the other side of the building, Jimmy had to make his way through a couple of hallways. As he rounded the corner he heard voices in the auditorium.

He stuck his head in and was horrified to see three kids snickering and taunting an 8th grade, mentally challenged student. They were throwing the boys' book back and forth, making him chase it. The boy was medium height with blonde hair. His eyes were beginning to glass over as he began to get more and more upset. His cries of "Gimme that" echoed off the auditorium walls. They were so sickening that it made Jimmy's stomach turn.

His anger arose as he raced down the aisle towards the bullies. They saw Jimmy coming and were petrified. He snatched the book from one of the kids, who froze instantly. "Real tough guys, huh? You wanna' take this book from me?" he thundered. Nobody moved. Just then, a teacher, hearing all the commotion entered the auditorium. He asked Jimmy what was going on and Jimmy relayed in full detail, much to the disappointment of the bullies. "Get to the principal's office NOW!" commanded the teacher. Jimmy asked if he could walk the boy back to his class.

The boy's name was Mark and he was new to the school having moved from out of town during the summer. Mark didn't say much when Jimmy tried to make conversation.

"People always make fun of me" he said sadly. But after some gentle prodding, Jimmy found out that Mark liked sports.

All of a sudden, Jimmy had a great idea! "I think we've found our team manager for baseball" he thought excitedly. Jimmy delivered Mark back to class and explained to his teacher what had happened. Jimmy gave Mark a big high five and told him that he would see him at lunch or recess.

Later in the day, Jimmy entered the cafeteria and looked for Mark. He saw the three bullies sitting together at a nearby table, laughing. They looked like three little rats he thought. All they needed was a tail and some whiskers. None of them had any friends and all they did was hang out with each other. A perfect trio.

Jimmy glared at them and their laughter quickly disappeared. Then, he saw Mark sitting at a table with his class, only he was all alone at the end of the table. He walked over and patted him on the back. "Hey, what are you doing sitting all by yourself?" he asked.

Mark shrugged his shoulders and said nothing. "You wanna' sit with me?" Mark smiled and nodded his head. "Let me get my lunch and we'll sit back there" he said, motioning to a table at the back of the cafeteria.

Jimmy found out that once he was comfortable, Mark was a VERY talkative person. He was a gold-medal-winning Special Olympian. He had a mom and older sister but no father. Being an only child with two wonderful parents, Jimmy felt a sudden case of sadness come over him.

After about 15 minutes together, Jimmy asked Mark if he liked baseball. Yeah, he LOVED baseball. Jimmy asked Mark if he would like to be the manager of the school baseball team. Mark was a bit hesitant at first because he thought people would make fun of him. Jimmy assured him that nobody would make fun of him and that he would be right there.

After lunch, Jimmy went to his coach and explained the situation. He thought that Mark would make an excellent team manager. The coach agreed.

Before he left school, he went to the office and got Mark's home number so he could call his mom to make sure it was ok. That night after dinner, he phoned Mark's mom. She told him that whatever he did for Mark today, she was very grateful, adding, "Mark hasn't been able to stop talking about you since he got home."

She also explained that she didn't think it was a good idea to have Mark as the manager as he was prone to having very bad temper tantrums, especially when teased. Jimmy assured her that nobody would make fun of him and that he would take full responsibility for Mark. He could even ride home after practice with Jimmy's mom and dad. It took some persuasion but Mark's mother finally agreed.

Jimmy introduced Mark at his first practice. Bobby, TJ and Sam made him feel right at home. Mark was painfully shy at first but once he felt comfortable, he was one of the guys. He was given a warm-up jacket and was expected to be in uniform for every game. He and Jimmy always played catch before practice and games. They both saw it as a pre-game ritual that nobody could interrupt.

Nobody cheered louder on the bench for Jimmy than Mark. He blew bubbles with the bubble gum Jimmy would give him and was the first to congratulate him when he crossed home plate. Mark would also take it upon himself to give the pre-game prep talk much to everyone's delight.

Mark and Jimmy's relationship really began to grow. They were together constantly and Mark adored him. They became "Jimbo" and "Marko." Jimmy looked upon him as the little brother he never had and was extremely protective as you could imagine.

It was never more evident when one of the junior high girls made the nasty remark to Jimmy: "Why he was wasting his time hanging out with a retard."

Candice Nettles was, in the mildest of terms, a self-centered, spoiled girl who took delight in putting down other people. She dressed in the best clothes and basically thought she was better than everyone. The girls that Candice hung around with had personalities that were almost identical to hers.

Jimmy was furious when he heard her cruel remark and told Candice in front of her friends that she had no clue when it came to compassion and understanding. "Perhaps if you weren't so stuck up, you could learn something from Mark" he said angrily. From that day forward, Jimmy never gave Candice Nettles the time of day.

With Jimmy's help and devotion, Mark slowly began to gain more confidence in everything he did. All of Jimmy's buddies took mark under their wings too.

After walking home with Mark from practice one day, Mark's mom told Jimmy that she had never seen her son happier. The baseball team went 10-1 for the season and Jimmy convinced mark that he was their good luck charm.

At his Special Olympics Track Meet in November, Jimmy and half the junior class had their own cheering section for Mark as he raced to a first-place finish in the 100-yard dash. Jimmy bounded down from the stands and his pals followed. Mark was so happy, he picked Jimmy right off his feet. Jimmy got goose bumps. When Mark received his first-place medal on the winner's platform, he gave Jimmy a big thumbs up.

Everyone went back to Mark's house for a pizza party. Mark relished in the attention, showing off his gold-medal as his new pals showered him with praise and high fives. Jimmy was bursting with pride for his buddy.

After a while, no one knew where Mark was. His mom went up to his room to find him sitting at his desk writing on a piece of paper. He told her he would be right down.

As everyone began to leave later, Mark pulled Jimmy aside and handed him a piece of paper and gave him a hug. On his way home with his pals, he opened the paper that was folded into four sections. He stopped under a streetlight to read it.

The note simply said, "Jimmy, you're the best friend I've ever had" signed Mark. The warmth that Jimmy felt at that moment was indescribable. His eyes began to fill up. He read it several more times before putting it back in his pocket. That night, before he went to bed, he taped Mark's note to his dresser.

Jimmy and Mark continued to be as close as brother's through high school. Mark was now officially one of the guys. Even Jimmy's girlfriend Samantha loved Mark. The three of them could be seen on the weekends hanging out or going for pizza. Jimmy would playfully remind Mark that Samantha was *his* girlfriend and to stay away. Mark would get so embarrassed that he turned red.

Samantha's friends would say hello to Jimmy in the hallway and he would blush first, then stick his chest out like a peacock. Mark was Jimmy's biggest fan at his soccer and basketball games and would sit and cheer proudly in the "rowdy" section surrounded by his buddies. Jimmy and the guys had given him a school cap and t-shirt that he cherished.

One day after basketball practice, Mark's mom invited Jimmy to the house for dinner. Jimmy arrived early and went up to check on Mark in his room. When he opened the door, his jaw hit the ground. He looked around the room and was amazed at what he saw! Mark had kept every article about Jimmy since he was in 8th grade. They were plastered over the walls! Even the notes and birthday cards that Jimmy had given him were there. Jimmy was completely blown away.

That night at dinner when Mark was in the other room, Mark's mom said to Jimmy, "You have no idea how much my son loves you, Jimmy Porter. I can never repay or thank you enough for what you have done for him."

Jimmy told her that he loved Mark like a brother and that he would always look out for him.

She then said quietly, "Jimmy, there's something I need to tell you about Mark." Jimmy felt uneasy as he looked at her. "Mark has degenerative heart disease and is not supposed to live past the age of 18. His heart is weak because of his mental and physical disabilities and it will only get worse."

The words hit Jimmy like a sledgehammer. He stared at Mark's mother. He simply could not believe it.

"We'll talk about it more tomorrow," she said as Mark came back into the room.

As Jimmy lay in bed that night, he couldn't help but be overcome with emotion and burst out crying. He put his pillow over his face and wailed like a wounded animal, choking and sobbing for over an hour.

As the months passed, Jimmy told no one of his conversation with Mark's mother and began to spend more and more time with his best friend. Nothing else mattered more than spending time with his buddy.

They were both seniors now. As Homecoming King, Jimmy made sure that Mark rode in the passenger seat of their car. Mark waved so much his arm ached.

At Christmas time, they sold trees for the school and wore Santa hats. The one day, Jimmy looked at Mark. He noticed that he looked thin and pale. Jimmy lectured him on eating healthy and getting plenty of sleep. He was also alarmed by Mark's sudden difficulty in breathing. He drove Mark home that night and told Mark's mother of his concern. "Mark's going to the doctor tomorrow for a checkup," she said.

The next day at practice, Jimmy was alarmed not to see Mark in the stands. He hurried to his house after practice. Mark's mom invited Jimmy in and told him that Mark was taking a nap. She told Jimmy the doctor said that Mark would really have to cut down on physical activities as he was just getting too weak.

Jimmy went up to Mark's room and opened the door quietly. He noticed Jimmy was having a very difficult time breathing. He went and sat down on a chair next to Mark's bed and looked at him.

He left at around 11pm that night while Mark was still sleeping. The next day, Jimmy phoned Mark's mom to see how he was doing.

"Mark won't be coming to school anymore Jimmy, he's just too weak," she said. Mark told her that he would be over after practice to visit. "He's been asking about you constantly," Mark's mother said.

Jimmy raced over to Mark's house after practice and was shocked to see an ambulance in the driveway. He felt an awful pit in his stomach and rushed inside. Paramedics had an oxygen mask on Mark and as he got closer to the stretcher he was on, Mark said quietly, "Jim-bo." Jimmy's eyes swelled as he yelled, "You're gonna' be OK buddy. You're gonna' be OK."

Jimmy followed the ambulance to the hospital and stayed with Mark's mother and sister in the waiting room. Two hours later, the doctor said they could see Mark. He had been moved to a room and all three stayed vigil at Mark's bedside.

At midnight, Mark took off his oxygen mask and looked at Jimmy. He spoke softly about the fun times they had in baseball and basketball and in school as his mother and sister looked on. "Jimbo, I love you buddy. You are my best friend in the whole world."

Jimmy held Mark's hand and said, "I love you too buddy. You are MY best friend in the world." They both held each other's hand's tightly. Mark closed his eyes and went to sleep. He died peacefully at 4:45am with his mother, sister and Jimmy holding hands.

In the days that followed there was a terrible silence. The silence swelled and roared, because silences can do that if what you want to hear isn't there and what you don't want to hear is everywhere.

Jimmy struggled with losing his best friend. He called Mark's mother and sister regularly to check on them. He moved through school like a zombie and lost much of his fire at practices and games.

Jimmy couldn't even talk to his parents about the loss of Mark. His only release was the sports he played. The running and the competition somehow eased the hurt. In everything he performed in, he always dedicated it to Mark. Slowly, the pain eased. It went from unbearable to bearable.

Jimmy began to look back on Mark's life and the impact that he had on people. How Mark brought so many of them together on the baseball team. How Jimmy and his friends would cheer like crazy at Mark's Special Olympics events. They all wanted the best for him. He remembered how much courage Mark showed throughout his life. He

thought of the wonderful times they shared;
walking home from games in the spring, hugging
him after his Gold Medal at The Special Olympics,
the Thanksgiving Parade and the fun they had
selling Christmas trees. It was going to be tough
without Mark, Jimmy thought. He wished they
could have had more time together, but was
thankful for the time they shared.

About a month after Mark had died, Jimmy
was in his room reading. He had just finished
reading when the phone rang. He picked it up. The
caller on the line caught Jimmy by surprise. The
tearful, soft voice on the other end said, "Jimmy,
this is Candice Nettles and I don't blame you if you
don't want to talk to me but *please* don't hang up."

Jimmy was silent.

"I want to tell you how sorry I am on your
loss of Mark" she said, her voice cracking. I know
you hate me for what I said about him last year but
I want to tell you how truly sorry I am."

"I don't hate you Candice," replied Jimmy.

"You have no idea how terrible I feel Jimmy. I am so sorry. I really am," she said crying.

"Thank you very much. It took a lot of courage to make this call Candice and I really appreciate it." They said good night and hung up the phone.

He looked at a picture of he and Mark on his dresser. He remembered something in a book he was reading about a year ago; An act of kindness towards someone else, no matter how big or small can make an everlasting impact in their lives. He smiled as he thought of Mark.

HUMOR

The boy cautiously approached his father as he read the evening paper.

"Dad, can I speak to you for a few minutes?" he asked.

"Sure John, come and sit down. What's on your mind?" said the father as he put down the paper.

"Well Dad" the boy began, "I'm going to be getting my license next month and I'd like to see if I can borrow the car from time to time. I'm sick and tired of walking to wherever I need to go."

The father looked at the boy for a few moments and said, "Now John, I knew this day would come and I've been thinking about this for a while and I'm going to be totally honest with you. I've been extremely disappointed with your lack of effort around this house." The boy stared at the father. "If you're going to have the privilege of using the car then I'm going to implement some standards that you need to adhere to."

"Like what?" the boy inquired.

"Well for example, your mother tells me that she constantly has to ask you to help her out around the house. You don't do anything around here and she's quite perturbed about that. I want you to begin helping out around the house and doing chores. Secondly, I want you to spend more time with your younger brother and sister. They look up to you so much and you treat them like they don't exist. Thirdly, your grades have gotten worse over the last year and it's been from lack of concentration and discipline. You need to bring those grades up to a solid "B" average. Number four, I want you to read more. Reading son, is the key to all education and can give you a tremendous foundation. Read more of the Bible too. Not so much for the spiritual sense but for the wonderful stories and examples it has. And lastly, you need to cut that hair of yours. You're a young man now and not a hippie."

The father arose from his chair and placed both his hands on the boy's shoulders. "So, we are clear on what you need to do to be able to use the car, correct?" he said. "Help your mother out, be a true Big Brother, improve your grades, read more and get a haircut. Now do we understand each other son?"

"Yes dad. I won't let you down" said the boy excitedly.

After one month, the boy came into the living room and sat down next to his father. "Can I talk to you dad?"

"Sure thing son. I've been wanting to talk to you and tell you how proud I am of you." said the father. The boy brightened. "Your mom says you're like a new man around the house, helping her out even when she doesn't ask you. I'm very pleased" praised the father. "And I've been watching you really take an interest in your brother and sister and that makes your mother and I very happy." The boy beamed. "And I'm so impressed at your grades. In a short time, you've risen to over a "B" average. That's just amazing, son."

The boy's chest puffed out.

"And I've seen you reading at night in your room and the books that you bring home from the library. That's just wonderful. But the only thing I'm disappointed in, John, is that you haven't got a haircut."

The boy rubbed his hands together nervously, looked down, then up at his father. "Well now dad, I knew you were going to say something about my hair, but I want you to know that I've been reading quite a bit of the Bible. And in the Bible, all the Apostles had long hair. EVEN Jesus had long hair dad."

The father looked at the boy and said, "You are EXACTLY right son. And they walked their behinds off everywhere they went!"

COMPASSION

Laura had been the top box office attraction at studio giant, Metro-Goldwyn-Mayer for several years. She was the little girl that everyone remembered from a famous classic movie. Because of the day-to-day pressures of performing and rehearsing, she became severely ill, lost weight and bordered on a nervous breakdown. She had also become addicted to pills and liquor.

The studios in those days were relentless and brutal in their treatment of child stars. Laura had made 27 pictures in 13 years! Feeling that she couldn't go on, she appealed to her manager. The studio boss reluctantly agreed.

The studio boss was a fearsome tyrant and ruled his stars by fear and fear alone. Laura was sent to a renowned hospital for thirteen weeks. It was a terribly difficult time for Laura as she hated leaving behind her small child, whom she adored and missed terribly.

While at the hospital, Laura was placed on a rigid schedule. Pills and liquor were withdrawn and lights went out in her room at 9pm every night and remained off whether she slept or not. She was fed three generous meals a day and slowly began to get her strength back.

After four weeks, the agony of withdrawal ended. Since Laura was weak and despondent and yearning for her child, the hospital doctors decided that some kind of "active therapy" would be good for her.

The hospital had an annex for mentally and physically challenged children. In those days, the children were labeled "retarded." It was suggested that Laura "give" an hour or two a day to the entertainment (storytelling, singing simple songs, etc.) of these children, many of whom had been there for twelve or thirteen years.

The experience was a traumatic one for Laura, remaining with her for years after and influencing her decision to, years later, star in another now famous movie in which she portrayed the teacher in a school for mentally and physically challenged kids.

All she would remember was the children's eyes. Laura was haunted in her lonely hours by the memory of her own child's wide, brown eyes. These mentally and physically challenged children – some in their late teens and early twenties but still no more than seven or eight – were unguarded in the desperate need to be loved that their eyes revealed.

Most of these children lived out their lives in institutions, and after the first year, parent's visits became farther and farther apart. Other family members seldom visited – so that when a parent died or left the area, the child was always waiting for that representative of outside love.

The children at the hospital responded immediately to Laura. They had seen her movies and she was familiar to them.

From the very first moment she entered the ward they waved and called "Hi" to her, thinking she was someone they knew well; for unable to retain the memory of a book or story or film for more than a few hours, they did story familiarity. Her warmth assured them they had not been mistaken. Laura was someone they knew and felt comfortable with. She represented their outside love.

One child – a small, dark-haired little girl not much older than her own child and with those same wide, brown eyes – resisted. Her gaze fixed and followed Laura all over the entire ward. But she remained huddled, totally withdrawn, her body wrapped about herself in a fetal position.

She had not spoken a word in the two years she had been on the ward, communicating with neither the other children or the staff. Rejected completely by her own family, she never had visitors.

It became the major point of each day for Laura to spend time with this little girl. She talked to her conversationally, expecting no reply and moving on to another story without stopping. She told her all about herself and her own child and about Hollywood. She sang nursery songs to her and getting braver and braver after a time, reached out and touched the child. The little girl listened but never returned an emotion, a word or touch. The staff was still hopeful and Laura continued.

The "active therapy" for the children worked wonders for Laura too and her health improved steadily. The migraines lessened, the depression lifted greatly and she was able to sleep.

After three months, though, the dreaded call came. The studio had ordered her back to work. Returning to work was a huge mistake, as the hospital felt Laura need at least another three months to fully recuperate.

Laura was reluctant but went along with the studio and prepared to leave the hospital. The last thing she did was to go to the ward and say goodbye to the mentally and physically challenged children.

The staff had prepared them for Laura's departure. The older ones dressed for the occasion, and each one presented her with some flowers from the hospital garden. But the little brown-eyed girl was not present. Laura went in search of her and found her on the last bed of the last ward.

Laura walked over and sat down on the edge of the bed. The child huddled there, staring at her with wide, sad dark eyes. It was truly heartbreaking for Laura and the moment held great meaning for her.

The child might have been mentally challenged, but she was sensitive enough to realize that she had been rejected and deserted. Her muteness was a defense, a wall against further rejection.

The staff briefed Laura on this problem. They had felt that Laura could break through to the child. Now Laura was in complete terror that if she left, the little girl would retreat even deeper into her own solitary confinement. Still, she could not do anything but reach out and try to draw the child into an embrace, for Laura was by natural instinct a maternal woman.

In an instant, the child broke out of the embrace, screaming and shouting Laura's name at the top of her lungs. The sound was bloodcurdling and all the other children and staff came running.

Then, throwing herself into Laura's arms, she clung fiercely and words, mostly unintelligible, poured from her between sobs. But Laura understood that the child did not want her to leave; and though she missed her train, she remained with the child for several hours until the storm had passed.

She sat there by her side until the child had fallen asleep. "I love you, I love you" the exhausted child said softly before closing her eyes.

"If you love me, you must promise me you'll talk to the doctors and nurses because they love you very much too," Laura replied.

The child slowly nodded her head as she drifted off to sleep.

How much does it really take to show someone compassion?

PATRIOTISM

In a classroom one afternoon, a pompous collegiate professor was lecturing his class of two hundred in a large auditorium.

"There is no God in the world that we live in," exclaimed the professor, an atheist.

A member of the class, a Marine sitting in the front row, listened intently. He had served his country well and had done three tours of duty in Afghanistan and had been awarded three Purple Hearts for his bravery along with numerous other medals.

As the professor continued to rant about there being no God, the Marine started to become angry. "If there is a God, then let him come and knock me off this podium that I stand on. Come on God, I'm waiting for you to knock me off this podium. KNOCK ME OFF," said the professor sarcastically.

The Marine bolted from his seat and rushed towards the professor. The startled professor froze as the Marine hit him so hard he knocked him out cold.

When the professor came to a couple of minutes later, he wobbled to his feet and saw the Marine sitting in his seat. The professor walked over and said, "Now why on earth did you do that to me young man?"

The Marine stood up and looked the professor directly in the eye and said, "Sir, I wanted you to know that God was busy today protecting our brave men and women that defend this country home and abroad. He was busy protecting them and our freedom so that people like you can say stupid things like that." GOD BLESS AMERICA!

THE ROCK

The president of this company had a well-known reputation for his poor treatment of his employees. He belittled them in public, verbally abused and often bullied them. Despite his success in business, he seemed to be an extremely unhappy, lonely man.

On this particular day, his new secretary was the recipient of his outburst. She had forgotten to include an important luncheon appointment with a client on his schedule. After screaming at her and embarrassing her, he promptly fired her on the spot. "You have one-hour to clean out your desk and get off these premises" he shouted. Through tears, she did just that as all the other stunned employees watched in silence.

He returned to his office, cursing under his breath and slammed the door. Calling the client on the phone, he immediately blamed the secretary for her "stupidity" and asked if they could meet in an hour later.

After rescheduling the appointment, he came out from his office with his usual scowl and glared at another worker and barked, "I'll be back in an hour. Take my messages for me." He typically was "telling" rather than "talking to."

As he entered the elevator, he frowned at the elderly woman who was there. He stood next to her looking straight ahead with even acknowledging her.

"A nice day outside" she said in a soft voice.

As the elevator came to a stop and the door opened he glared at her through clenched teeth and said, "NOT on the inside!"

He got into his Porsche and roared out of the garage cursing as he came to a traffic light. "Traffic is going to be brutal on the main highway" he thought so he decided to take a shortcut through the suburb.

He rode along at top speed when he looked down at his watch. BAM! He brought the car to a screeching halt. Had he hit something?

He looked left and right then got out of the car. He looked over at the passenger door and there was a dent the size of a baseball just below the door handle. "What the......? He thought.

Then he turned around to find a little boy, no more than ten years old. The boy was frightened and stood there motionless holding something in his right hand. It was a rock.

Suddenly, the man began to put two and two together. He shouted, "Did you throw something at my car?" The boy just looked at him. "DID YOU? He screamed.

The boy was now terrified and nodded his head slowly. The man was beside himself and started to walk towards the boy. "Do you know how much this car is worth....What do you think you were doing....You're going to pay for this, you little punk, and I'm calling the cops and will press charges against you!"

The young boy didn't move but was shaking. His lips quivered as his eyes filled up. "But nobody would stop" he said barely above a whisper. "Not one person."

The man was now in front of the boy about two feet away. "What are you talking about, you little derelict?" he said sarcastically.

Through tears the boy said, "I tried to wave people down but they wouldn't stop. The just kept going by."

The exasperated man snapped, "Why on earth would you want people to stop? Throwing a rock at someone's car is NOT what you do when you want them to stop their vehicle."

The boy turned around and began to walk away from the man. "HEY! Where do you think you're going?"

The boy said nothing but gestured for the man to follow him for about 20 yards. There was a huge hedge about 20 feet long and ten feet high that the boy stopped in front of.

"Where the heck are you....?" the man stopped dead in his tracks at the end of the hedge. His heart sank and his mouth got dry.

Lying on the ground was a child next to his wheelchair. The boy looked sadly at the man and said, "Nobody would stop, mister. I was wheeling my older brother home from a friend's house and turned his chair too much and he fell out. I'm not strong enough to pick him up. I've been pleading with people to stop but they kept going right by me. Do you see? I'll pay you for the damage mister but please don't call the police on me."

The man swallowed hard and stared at the boy for about 15 seconds. "Not to worry son, you did the right thing."

He then went over, picked up the boy lying on the ground and gently placed him back in his wheelchair giving him a pat on the head. He watched as the boy wheeled his brother down the street and disappeared out of sight.

Things in our life don't really become that important until we see or do things that really are.

LOVE

A farmer had a bunch of puppies that he wanted to sell so he nailed a sign on the fence post at the entrance of his property. As he finished, he felt a tug on his pants. He looked down to find a small boy about seven years.

The boy said, "sir, I want to buy one of your puppies."

The farmer chuckled and replied, "Son, these puppies had very expensive parents and they are a top-quality breed. I don't think you can afford them."

The boy reached into his pocket and took out a handful of change. "I got 39 cents. Will that get me a look?"

The farmer nodded his head and called out, "Dolly!"

Out of the doghouse on the other side of the fence came a puppy, followed by three more. The boy's eyes filled with delight as he pressed his face against the fence and watched the puppies run towards the farmer, jumping and bouncing along.

Then, another puppy emerged from the doghouse. He was much smaller than the other pups and ran with a slight limp. He certainly wasn't as fast as the others.

The boy looked at the farmer and said excitedly, "That's the one I want."

The farmer knelt down next to the boy and said, "Now son, you don't want THAT puppy. He can't keep up with the other puppies and certainly won't be able to keep up with you."

The boy looked at the farmer with his big brown eyes and reached down to pull up his pant leg. He revealed a thick, steel brace that came up over his knee.

"You see mister," said the boy. "I can't keep up with the other kids either and I thought that maybe we could help each other."

The farmer, with tears in his eyes, reached over the fence and picked up the little puppy and placed it in the boy's hands.

An enormous smile came across the boy's face. "How much do I owe you mister?"

The farmer looked at the boy and said softly, "No Charge."

The boy asked why and the farmer patted him on the head and said, "because there's no charge for love."

TEDDY

Miss Campbell was a fourth-grade elementary school teacher. Her devotion to her craft had earned her the admiration and respect of her colleagues and she was liked tremendously by her students.

At the beginning of each year, she enjoyed reading the progress reports of her student's history from first to fourth grade. Today though, something was bothering her about one of her students. The young boy was named Teddy and she could not understand why the child was so unmotivated and lethargic. He came to school almost in a daze and his appearance was quite disheveled.

She picked up his folder from the stack on her desk and began to read. Teddy's 1st grade teacher had written: "Teddy is a bright and cheerful young boy and should do very well in elementary school."

His 2nd grade teacher wrote: "Teddy is doing well but is severely bothered by his mother's illness."

Miss Campbell read further and her heart broke when she read Teddy's 3rd grade teacher's comments: "Teddy is completely out of sorts with the death of his mother and doesn't get any help at home from his alcoholic father."

In all her years of teaching, Miss Campbell had never felt this type of emotion towards one of her students. Right then and there, she vowed to use everything she had to bring out the absolute best in Teddy and get him back on his feet again.

It was no easy task, as Teddy had totally withdrawn from everything. Miss Campbell worked with him, encouraged, applauded and, at times, gently pushed him to do his best.

Slowly, Teddy began to emerge from his shell. He was developing new-found confidence and for the first time all year, Miss Campbell saw a smile come across Teddy's face.

At Christmas time, all the other students had brought in presents for their teacher. They all were neatly wrapped with beautiful, ornate bows on them.

Teddy brought his present in a paper shopping bag that he had taped himself. The other children giggled as he came up to his teacher's desk.

A stern look to the class by Miss Campbell immediately made the giggles disappear. When she opened it, the teacher found a half-filled bottle of perfume along with a beautiful pearl necklace. She made the biggest deal out of the gifts and put a dab of the perfume on her neck and wrist. She praised Teddy for his kindness.

After school that day, Miss Campbell was at her desk correcting some papers when she heard a knock at the doors. She looked up to find Teddy. Inviting him in to sit down she asked if everything was OK.

"I have to tell you something Miss Campbell. May I stand?"

"Why of course you can," she replied.

Teddy looked down at the ground for a moment then looked up and said, "Miss Campbell, I want you to know that when you put that perfume on today, you smelled just like my mom."

The emotion that engulfed Miss Campbell's body at that instant was so powerful and sudden that she let out a soft whimper. Walking around her desk as her eyes filled with tears, she hugged Teddy hard and whispered, "Thank you, sweet Teddy."

Teddy's performance improved dramatically and he and Miss Campbell developed a fabulous relationship. Through her caring and kindness, she had broken down the wall that Teddy had put up.

When he graduated from 4th to 5th grade, Teddy wrote a note to Miss Campbell that said simply; "Miss Campbell, you are the best teacher I've ever had."

Every year until he graduated high school, Teddy always took the time to drop a quick note to his mentor and with every note, he penned the exact same closing line; "Miss Campbell, you are the best teacher I've ever had." This continued through his college years and through graduate school.

Then one day, after she had retired, Miss Campbell received a letter from Teddy. He was studying to be a doctor. Miss Campbell was overjoyed!

She was even more thrilled several years later when she was invited to Teddy's wedding. As she sat in the church pew she looked at how handsome Teddy was. More importantly, she could not believe what he had accomplished when the odds were so stacked against him. He was now Dr. Theodore Smith.

At the wedding reception, Teddy brought his new bride to meet Miss Campbell. Introducing his wife to Miss Campbell he called her his greatest mentor and inspiration. He then looked at her and froze for several seconds.

Miss Campbell had worn his mother's pearl necklace! She told Teddy, "Your mom is right here with you today in spirit," as she pointed to her heart. They both gave each other a big hug.

About 2 years later, Teddy called Miss Campbell and told her that he raised funds to build a wing on a new cancer center in his hometown. It would be in his mother's memory. He was extremely happy and wanted Miss Campbell to attend the ceremony.

As she sat by the fire that evening, she smiled as she thought of all Teddy had achieved and it warmed her heart immensely.

No matter how down in life you may be, you can always find the right road with persistence, determination and a wonderful mentor that truly believes in you.

KNOWING JUST HOW GOOD
YOU REALLY ARE

The manager of a well-known venue in New York City had tried to book an extremely talented pianist and for months his efforts were in vain. Then, finally, he was able to land the young man for a spring concert. The manager went to great lengths to publicize and promote the event and his efforts were rewarded that evening with a sold-out house.

The pianist played unbelievably for two solid hours and had the audience in the palm of his hand. After his last song, he received a tremendous ovation that lasted for a number of minutes.

During the applause, the manager ran to the wings and exclaimed excitedly to the pianist, "YOU NEED TO GO BACK OUT AND DO AN ENCORE!"

The pianist shook his head. The manager said "What do you mean? LISTEN TO THAT CROWD! ENCORE! ENCORE!"

The pianist replied, "No, it wasn't good enough."

The manager said, "To the contrary my boy. EVERYONE is standing!"

The young man said, "Not everyone is standing."

The manager said, "Believe me, EVERYONE is standing and clapping."

The pianist said, "Not everyone is standing sir. See the man in the back row. He is sitting." "The man obviously DOES NOT know his music" the manager shot back in a disgusted voice.

"Yes, he DOES" said the boy confidently. "That's my teacher."

MAKING SOMEONE'S LIFE

Over the course of my fifty-two years, I have been privileged to meet some extraordinary people. One of those would have to be the late actor Ed Lauter. Ed's career spanned over fifty years and I was terribly saddened when he lost a courageous battle with Mesothelioma in 2014.

I first met Ed back in 1995 when I was an aspiring publicist for the Lee Solters Company in Beverly Hills, CA. We were introduced by a mutual friend, another wonderful man, Hollywood agent Tino Barzie. I liked Edward Matthew Lauter instantly and we became good friends. We maintained that relationship even when I left Hollywood and moved back to Massachusetts.

Ed worked with some giants in the movie industry; Burt Lancaster, Charlton Heston, Burt Reynolds, Charles Bronson and Clint Eastwood just to name a few. Needless to say, he was a master storyteller with endless stories to boot. When I returned to Cape Cod, I landed a job at ESPN Radio as an announcer. This brought me into a wide, new world of sports. One of the best things of working at ESPN Radio in my capacity was that I received many invitations to play in celebrity golf tournaments all over the country.

One in the late 90's was in my own back yard; The Ocean Spray Celebrity Golf Classic. I recommended Ed to the organizers and they quickly agreed that they would like to have Ed as a celeb guest. To my amazement, Ed agreed even though he picked up a club only once in his life.

The four-day tourney was an absolute ball and the second day everyone was one their own. I met Ed at the cabana bar resort around 3pm. The next thing I knew, we were surrounded by people wanting to shake Ed's hand, take a picture or grab an autograph. I sat back and watched Ed work his magical personality with imitations and stories.

One, in particular, was quite profound. Ed enjoyed a fabulous, 40+ year relationship with

Frank Sinatra Jr. He told the story about the time he took his wife at the time and his mother (a HUGE Big Frank fan) to see Ole' Blue Eyes at The Sands Hotel in Vegas in the late 1970's. Tickets came courtesy of young Frank and the seats were front row, front and center. As an added treat, Big Frank even introduced Ed as one of the great character actors of our time (a gentleman by the name of Alfred Hitchcock also shared the exact sentiments) much to the delight of Ed's mom, Mary.

After the concert in which Frank was in exceptional voice, the trio went backstage to thank Frank Jr. for the tickets. Without batting an eye, Frank Jr. invites Ed, his wife and Mom to dinner with "The Old Man."

Everyone is simply blown away by the junior Sinatra's kindness including Mary Lauter. They arrive at the Sinatra VIP Room at The Sands and it is palatial. For the next three hours, food and drink come to the party of thirty like a Roman

Festival. Big Frank is seated at the head of the table and is good spirits as his concert was superb.

Towards the end of the evening, Ed passes the word to Frank Jr. that they are going to get going and would like to say thank you for the hospitality and introduce his wife and mother to Big Frank. Word comes back that it's ok. As they approach the head of the table, Big Frank is now drinking a snifter of Sambuca. Ed approaches and Frank greets him warmly as the elder Sinatra always liked Ed.

After some pleasantries, Ed introduces his wife and mother Mary. Mary Lauter goes up to Big Frank and like a little schoolgirl says, "Mr. Sinatra, I saw you at the Statler Theater in Pittsburgh, Pennsylvania in 1952 and you were absolutely amazing."

The table has now grown silent as all eyes are on The Chairman of The Board. Sinatra looks down, swirls his drink around and takes a sip, setting the glass down he takes Mary Lauter's hand for effect and looks directly at her with those huge blue eyes and says, "Mary, The Statler Theater, Pittsburgh, 1952. I was on stage. You were in the front row down to my left and you were the best looking dame in the whole place."

Edward Matthew Lauter said that right then and there, "My mother completely wet her pants!"

I said to him later when we were alone, "Eddie, how many times did Sinatra use that line?" He said, "Wayno, probably ten million. But the ONE time he used it to my mother, she talked about that right up until the day she died.

It doesn't make a difference who you are in this world or what your stature is, it only takes a few minutes to leave someone with a little bit of kindness and make their day.

WHAT IS TIME REALLY WORTH?

The young, 8-year old boy sat at the kitchen table with his father while his mother served dinner. He was totally preoccupied and was doodling on a pad of paper, completely oblivious to his father's questions on how school went today.

As the mother sat down to the table, the boy finished doodling and stared at his dad. The boy began talking about how other kids at school were bragging about their dad's. "That's nice" was all the father would say as now he was becoming oblivious to his son's banter.

After a long silence, the boy said, "hey dad, how much money do you make a year?' The father looked on with a completely stunned look. Several seconds later the look turned to anger. "That's none of your business son," he snapped. "I work extremely hard to put a roof over your head and your mother's and I work hard to put food on the table. That's all you need to

75

know. What I make a year is NONE OF YOUR BUSINESS!" With that, he banished the boy to his room.

The father had not had a very good day at work and his patience was quite strained. His wife looked at him but said nothing. After playing with his food, he pushed his plate away angrily and went into the living room to read the evening paper.

After about ten minutes, he threw the paper down and stared straight ahead, finally realizing that he had been a little tough on his 8-year old son. He arose from the chair and headed upstairs to the boy's room. Opening the door, he found his son lying on his back looking at the ceiling. The dad apologized and tried to explain to the boy that young 8-year old boys shouldn't be asking questions about what a parent makes a year.

"I'm sorry dad" said the boy and the father gave him a big hug and told him to get ready for bed.

The next morning, a Saturday, the little boy came cheerfully downstairs for breakfast and noticed that his father was already at the table reading the paper.

"Going to watch some cartoons today" the boy exclaimed.

"That's good" said the father.

The boy obviously had something on his mind as he began to eat his cereal. The father continued to read his paper as the boy finally spoke, "Hey Dad, how much do you make a week?" The father could not believe what he was hearing and as he stared at his young son, his blood began to boil. "What did you just say? he said between clenched teeth.

"I said" the boy said softly, "how much do you make a week?

"What did I tell you last night? the father shot back. "I think you need to go to your room again so that it sinks in this time, NOW GO!" He shouted.

77

As the father worked in the yard during the day, it again weighed on him how hard he had been on his son. He kept reasoning with himself, "So what if he asks you how much you make. It's good for him to know so that he can become fiscally responsible. Goodness sake, he's ONLY EIGHT YEARS OLD!"

The father went inside and showered, then he went into his son's room and found him lying on his bed reading a book. As he sat down on the side of the bed and patted him on his head, the boy simply could not resist.

"Dad, I know you got upset when I asked you how much you make a year and how much you make a week and I'm sorry that I upset you. But could I just ask you one more question, please?"

"Sure son, go right ahead. I think I've been overreacting a little bit."

"Ok," said the boy, "but you promise you won't get mad?"

"I promise" said the dad quietly.

"Alright dad, how much do you make an hour?" The father simply couldn't believe what he was hearing. He wasn't upset anymore but extremely curious why his son wanted to know so much about his salary.

"You know what son," said the father, "if you really want to know, Dad makes about fifty dollars an hour. Are you satisfied?"

Upon hearing that the boy's eyes lit up like a Christmas tree. He got on his knees and through aside his pillow. The father was amazed to see a bunch of change and lots of dollar bills all crumpled up. "Help me count it dad, help me count it" the boy yelled.

The father hurriedly helped the boy count his money and proclaimed that the boy had saved Fifty-Four Dollars and seventeen cents.

REALLY? REALLY?" shouted the boy.

"Yes, son. Now tell me, why are you so excited?" A big, smile came across the boy's face and his eyes opened real wide.

"Now," he said, "I have enough money to buy an hour of your time."

We can never get back lost time with our children. EVERY moment is precious.

THE IMPACT BUTTON

An executive of a major company was sitting at his desk one Friday afternoon when his secretary buzzed him and said that he had a visitor. The man was up to his eyeballs in work and was quite annoyed. He was about to answer his secretary when the door to his office opened and there stood a young man with a wide grin on his face.

"Good afternoon Mr. Johnson, my name is Jim Smith and I'm one of your interns here at the company. I am graduate of Purdue University with a major in business" he said while extending his hand. "May I sit down?" The young man asked.

The president sat dumbfounded as the young man continued to speak at a feverish pace.

"Do you know what today is Mr. Johnson?"

"Friday" deadpanned the executive.

"Ah, yes, it is," said the boy, "but more importantly, today is National Impact Day in corporations all over America."

The executive stared with a curious look on his face. He simply could not believe the Chutzpah of this young man. Coming into his office unannounced, without an appointment, sitting here lecturing me on some stupid National Impact thing.

"Listen," said the executive now exasperated. "I have a great deal of work to do and quite frankly, you are prohibiting me from doing it. Go see my secretary and she'll be able to help you." he said in a dismissive manner.

Not to be outdone, the young man pulled a medium-sized button from his suitcoat and handed it to the executive.

"This is for you sir. Today is National Impact Day and I want you to know that I've been working at this company the last six months and you, more than anyone, have made a great impact on me."

The executive stared at the young man in disbelief. "What? You've got to be kidding me."

"No sir" exclaimed the young man, "I'm VERY serious. I have watched you since I began at this company, Mr. Johnson, and though at times you can be tough and stubborn, I believe that you generally care for people and want them to succeed. You are a driven man and I think that makes people around you better, especially me."

Almost apologetically, the man said in almost a whisper, "You see, my father was extremely tough on me and........" his voice trailed off.

With that, the boy arose from his chair, shook the executive's hand and went out the door as quickly as he came in.

"Thanks for this son," he called softly after the boy. For the rest of the afternoon, the executive kept looking at the button he had placed on his desk. At times, he would pick it up, admire it, even pin it on his shirt. Finally, after a couple of hours, he couldn't take it anymore and told his secretary that he was taking the remainder of the day off and heading home.

He packed his briefcase with work for the weekend and put his Impact Button in his shirt pocket. He arrived home with an intense euphoria about him. Rushing through the front door, he called out to see if anyone was home.

"I'm in my room" came the reply from the executive's teenage son.

Almost running up the stairs, the man burst into the room. The son was on his bed doing homework.

"What did I do WRONG now dad?" said the boy in a somber tone.

As the man went over to sit next to his son, he glanced on his night table and saw a letter that was addressed "TO DAD."

Plopping down on the bed, the father said excitedly to the boy, "Son, do you know what today is?"

The boy looked up from his homework and said, "What DIDN'T I do dad?"

"Son, you didn't do anything wrong. Do you know what today is?"

The boy shrugged, "Friday?"

"No, today is NATIONAL IMPACT DAY all over the country!" The father could barely contain his excitement. "And this is for you," he said as he pulled the button from his shirt pocket. "I want you to know how much of an impact you have made on me son....on me and your mother. We couldn't be prouder of you", he said with emotion.

After pausing for a few moments, he said, "By the way, what's that letter on your night table? It's not Father's Day and it certainly is not my birthday. What's up?"

Holding the button in his hand, the boy's eyes began to fill up and he began to cry in heavy sobs. The father was startled by the reaction and reached over and hugged his son. The boy returned the hug with such force that the father almost had trouble breathing.

"Hey pal, it's OK, this is a happy moment. The button is a GOOD thing." The boy kept crying and hugging his father ever so tightly. "Hey buddy, if you had a gift certificate for me, I'm sorry I ruined it. Really sorry."

The son now gently pulled away from the father and looked directly in eyes. "Dad, that was my suicide note."

At that moment, every bit of life was completely sucked out of the father and it was as if someone hit him in his chest with a sledgehammer. The only reply that he could muster and that was barely above a whisper was, "Why?"

"Dad," said the boy, "everything I do is ALWAYS wrong. I'm NEVER good enough, I can ALWAYS do better, be better. You NEVER tell me that you love me. The only time you speak to me is to tell me what I've done wrong. You treat me as though I was one of your employees."

One can only imagine the life lesson the father received that day. Our children are NOT perfect. Don't ever expect them to be. The results could be tragic.

FIRST IMPRESSIONS

A young couple were given one of the most precious gifts in the entire world when they welcomed a healthy baby girl into the world a few years after they were married. The daughter brought tremendous joy to the couple, especially the mother.

When the girl reached the age of six, she began to notice that her mother's hands looked quite different. The skin was almost raw in some places and they looked as if they had been burned. When the girl asked her mother about her hands, the mother simply said that she had been careless around the stove and that her hands were burned by some hot water, adding, that you always need to be careful around the stove.

When the daughter reached the age of nine, she began having friends over the house. She developed a habit of running home from the bus stop, going upstairs in her mother's room and retrieving a pair of white gloves that she would bring downstairs and make her mother put on. She never said to the mother directly that she was embarrassed by her hands and the mother said nothing.

This same scenario took place with future sleepovers, birthday parties and the daughter's prom. She was never completely comfortable until she saw that her mother had her white gloves on.

Over the years, the mother never uttered a word of protest or appeared angry or upset.

The day the daughter was married, the biggest day of her life to date, she wasn't concerned about her dress or the wedding, she was only concerned that the mother had her white gloves on and she made sure to remind her mother every chance she got.

Several years after the daughter got married, she too had given birth to a beautiful baby girl. One summer when the child was four years old, the daughter and her husband spent a weekend with her parents.

On a lovely summer evening, the grandmother was out on the porch reading stories to her granddaughter. After a while, the inquisitive little girl noticed how mangled her grandmother's hands were and asked what was wrong with them.

As the young child began to stroke her grandmother's hands, the grandmother said she would tell the little girl but she would have to keep it a secret and not tell anyone. The little girl promised and leaned back on her grandmother's chest as the old woman explained.

When the girl's mommy was just a baby, grandpa used to travel quite a bit as this was part of his job. It was three weeks before Christmas and grandpa was traveling, so grandma was home alone with your mommy. The house was beautifully decorated with lights and ornaments.

At around 2 am in the early morning, grandma was awakened by the smell of smoke. She jumped out of bed and raced down the hallway to your mommy's room where smoke was coming out. She opened the door and saw that the Christmas lights had caught fire to the curtain, right next to your mommy's bed and parts of the curtain were on fire inside your mommy's crib. Grandma rushed over and with her hands, put the flames out and scooped up your mommy and brought her to safety.

In telling this story, the grandmother had no idea that the daughter was in the next room. One can only imagine how the daughter felt at being embarrassed and ashamed by her mother's hands all those years. Those same hands, that were used to save her life. And over those years, because of the intense love the mother had for her daughter, she never said a word.

THE BOWL

The young couple were having an argument and it wasn't going well. The couple's 4-year-old son was in the next room playing (and listening). The wife wanted her 85-year-old father to come and live with them as he simply could no longer be by himself. The husband brought up the idea of a nursing home and the wife was completely against it.

"Why would I put my father in a place like that when he can come live with us? I will NOT put my father in a nursing home" she said adamantly.

The young son came and said he wanted grampa to come live with them too, much to the chagrin of the husband. The husband gave in but was not a happy camper. He and the wife did not speak for over a week.

The grandfather was delighted to be able to see his daughter and grandson every day. His highlights were watching his grandson play and reading to him.

Through every meal, the husband seethed until one day he exploded at his wife after dinner. "Your father's manners at the table are atrocious! He talks with his mouth full, spills his drinks and has dropped three plates on the floor since he came to live with us. I gave this a chance but this is utterly ridiculous!!! I can't take it anymore."

The wife pleaded with her husband and promised to help her father with his table etiquette. The husband said the old man could stay but would have to eat his meals in another room away from the family.

So, there he sat, every meal, in another room by himself. The old man was relegated to eating at a small card table with a plastic bowl and plastic utensils. He said nothing and never complained as he ate in silence. One night during dinner, the little grandson looked at his grandfather and thought he could see a tear running down the old man's cheeks.

One day after work, the father came home. Hanging up his coat, he sat down next to his young son who was playing on the floor. Giving him a big hug, he inquired as to what the boy was building.

"I'm making a plastic bowl for you and mommy to eat out of when you get old," he said happily.

The words hit the father like a ton of bricks. He said nothing as he stared straight ahead for several minutes. Clearing his throat, he went into the kitchen to talk with his wife.

That night, before dinner was served, the husband went into the next room, put his arm around his father-in-law and lead him back to the table. And for the rest of the old man's life, the son-in-law never cared if anything was spilled or broken.

A powerful lesson in compassion and respect.

PERSPECTIVE IN OUR LIFE

The phone is something that we use as a tool. It's a form of communication. The phone brings us happiness and joy. The phone also can be the bearer of bad news and tragedy.

I received a phone call from my son Spencer several years ago when he was a senior at Gordon College. Spen has always been a bright, intelligent, cheerful boy with a fabulous personality. I have been extremely proud of his accomplishments and achievements over the years. Equally, he is what every big brother should be: kind, caring and a role model.

When my cell phone rang that night around 10pm, I saw Spen's name come up on speed dial. I was happy to take the call and didn't think it unusual that my son would be calling me at that time.

But, after 5 seconds, I knew something was wrong by the tone of Spen's voice. I can still hear those awful words like it was yesterday, "I HAVE BEEN DIAGNOSED WITH CANCER." These are the words that no parent wants to ever hear from their child. It shook me to the core.

We spoke for a long time that night and I can remember not wanting to hang up the phone. I wanted desperately to go back to the day's when Spencer was a little kid, how we played soccer and baseball, how we used to go Elf Hunting around right before Christmas and how we went fishing. All this was a blur as my mind raced a thousand miles a minute. I didn't sleep at all and awoke early.

Spencer came home and I met him for lunch. I immediately placed a call to good friend Dr. Bob, a highly-respected cancer doctor. Dr. Bob was beyond magnificent as he gave Spen an insight on the type of cancer that he had (testicular), assured him that everything was going to be just fine and that is was HIGHLY CURABLE.

My son and I drove around for over an hour and I did my best to try and let him know that he was going to get through this with flying colors. Then, with words I'll NEVER forget, he looked at me and said with extreme confidence, "I'm really going to enjoy beating this thing. It's not going to get the best of me."

The motivational-speaking father was simply at a loss for words. I could not believe my son was already in "Battle Mode." he could have felt sorry for himself, could have blamed God or looked for excuses. Absolutely not.

Spen went through the horrific trials of Chemotherapy for eight awful weeks. He lost his hair and a bit of hearing, and his taste buds were affected.

He had some AMAZING friends that stood by him and helped him through this God-awful ordeal. One in particular was his summertime boss, Jim, who owns a local friend seafood place in Falmouth, MA.

Because of the sickness that Chemo brings on, Spen had to miss a few weeks of work. Upon returning, Jim called him into his office. My son thought he was going to be fired. Jim handed him an envelope with the three weeks' salary, plus the tips he would have made. Jim is a mensch and is unequivocally one of the kindest and most generous people you will ever meet.

I tell this story a great deal and every time I tell it, it warms my heart more and more. Spen made it through Chemo and battled all the side effects. Through all this, he never lost that wonderful personality and kept his strong belief in God. To me, there is nothing greater in life than when a doctor pronounces your child cancer free.

When speaking at a USA Hockey Clinic a couple of years ago, I made that statement to around 400 youth hockey coaches. I said that if anyone in that room could tell me of something greater, to please see me after my presentation.

As I received thanks from coaches after I was finished, a young man in his late 20's greeted me and said, "Mr. Soares. I know of something that is greater."

"And that is?" I asked.

He replied, "When your mother is cancer free." The young man's mother had battled cancer for four years and was now in remission. Powerful.

I'm happy to report that my son Spencer is cancer free. He makes the routine checkups and his health is great. He was married this past July to a wonderful girl and they reside in Missouri.

Never wait to get "perspective" in life. Appreciate what you have every day and never miss an opportunity to hug your children and tell them that you love them.

About the Author

Wayne Soares is an actor, inspirational speaker, comic and author.

Last year, the former ESPN Radio Broadcaster starred in two films; the crime drama "Snitches" and The mob comedy "The Curse of Don Scarducci" with Alec Baldwin.

Wayne continues to devote a great deal of time to entertaining our troops both home and abroad and has brought laughter to our military men and women in Afghanistan, Iraq, London, South Korea and Germany. He and his talented cast are currently touring the country with their new variety show "A Salute to Our Military."

Wayne was recently named spokesman for Boston Red Sox Hall of Famer Jason Varitek's Pitching in For Kid's Foundations new anti-bullying campaign, Be Kind, Always and his message has had a profound impact on thousands of youth across the country.

Wayne is the immensely proud father of three children and a huge supporter of The Special Olympics, The Dana Farber and The American Cancer Society.

Also Available From Summerland Publishing

The Big Game" by Wayne Soares is a wonderful book about how a young boy's dream turns into reality as he readies himself for his team's championship game. Tommy's ability to perform well is highlighted by the important key steps of concentration, preparation and good sportsmanship.

US$14.95/CAN$19.95　　　　　ISBN: 978-0-9824870-2-0

"The Power of Your Words and Actions" by Wayne Soares contains a superb collection of true life experiences which relate to how our words and actions affect everything we do in life, as well as others around us. The stories are heart-warming, and most readers will easily relate to many of them as they have no doubt experienced similar events in their own lives.

US$14.95/CAN$19.95　　　　　ISBN: 978-0-9795444-0-8

Order from:
summerlandpublishing.com, barnesandnoble.com,amazon.com or find it in your favorite bookstore!
Email SummerlandPubs@aol.com for more information.
Summerland Publishing, 887 Hanson Street,
Bozeman, MT 59718